POCKET · PUFFINS

For Susan and for Ava

Puffin Books, Penguin Books Ltd, Harmondsworth, Middlesex, England
Viking Penguin Inc., 40 West 23rd Street, New York, New York 10010, U.S.A.
Penguin Books Australia Ltd, Ringwood, Victoria, Australia
Penguin Books Canada Limited, 2801 John Street, Markham, Ontario, Canada L3R 1B4
Penguin Books (N.Z.) Ltd, 182–190 Wairau Road, Auckland 10, New Zealand

Puffin/Moonlight
First published in the United Kingdom by World's Work Ltd 1975
Text and illustrations copyright © Anita Lobel, 1975
Published in Pocket Puffins 1987 in association with Moonlight Publishing Ltd,
131 Kensington Church Street, London W8

Printed in Italy by La Editoriale Libraria

KING
ROOSTER,
QUEEN HEN

by Anita Lobel

POCKET PUFFINS

Once there lived
a rooster and a hen.

They pecked and scratched
in the ground.
They were very happy.

But one day the rooster said,
"I do not want to live
on this farm any more.
I want to go to the city.
When we get there, I will be king
and you will be my queen."

"We will need a carriage,"
said the hen.

"That is true," said the rooster.
The rooster and the hen
pecked and scratched in the
ground.

They found an old shoe.

"Cock-a-doodle-do!" cried the
rooster.

"Now we have a carriage."

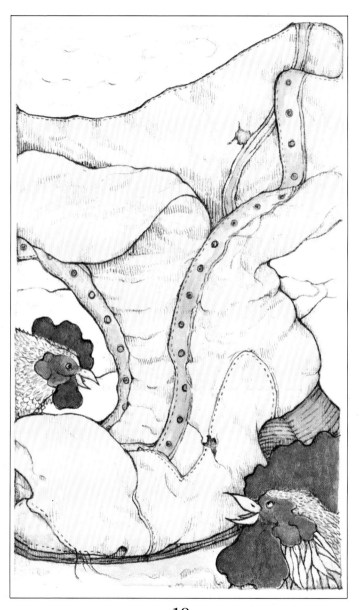

"We will need some horses,"
said the hen.
"That is true," said the rooster.
The rooster and the hen
pecked and scratched again.

They found a nest
of field mice.
"Cock-a-doodle-do!"
cried the rooster.
"Now we have horses."

"We will need bits and reins,"
   said the hen.
"That is true," said the rooster.
   Again the rooster and the hen
   pecked and scratched.
   They found some sticks
   and some string.
"Cock-a-doodle-do!"
   cried the rooster.
"Now we have the bits
   and the reins."

The rooster and the hen
tied the mice to the shoe.
They drove away from the farm.
Before long they met a sparrow.
"Where are you going?" she asked.
"To the city to be king and queen,"
said the rooster.
"May I come with you?"
said the sparrow.
"What can you be?"
asked the rooster.

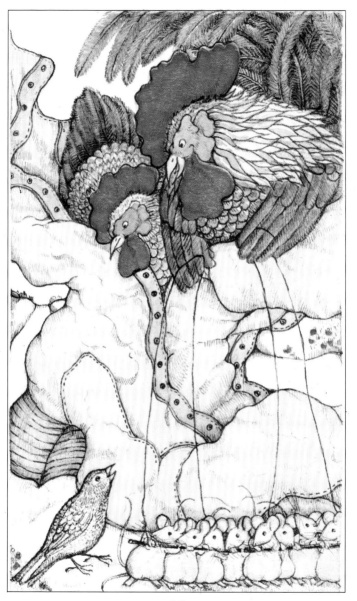

"I can be the queen's maid,"
said the sparrow.

"That is a fine idea,"
said the hen.
"Hop in!" said the rooster
to the sparrow.
"Cock-a-doodle-do!"
The rooster and the hen
made room in the shoe
for the sparrow.
The mice travelled on.

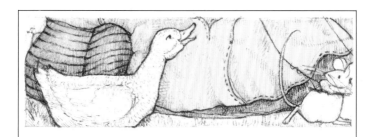

Soon they met a duck.
"Where are you going?"
she asked.
"To the city
to be king and queen,"
said the rooster.
"May I come with you?"
said the duck.
"The queen has a maid,"
said the rooster.
"What can you be?"

"I can be the cook,"
said the duck.

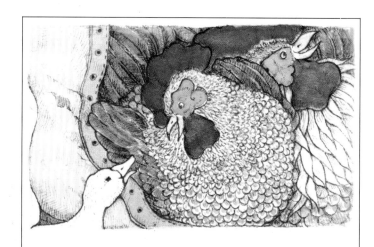

"That is a fine idea," said the hen.
"Jump in!" said the rooster
to the duck. "Cock-a-doodle-do!"
The rooster, the hen
and the sparrow
made room in the shoe
for the duck.
The mice travelled on.

Then they met a crow.

"Where are you going?"

he asked.

"To the city to be king and queen,"

said the rooster.

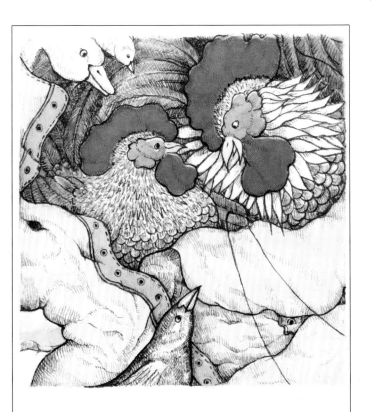

"May I come with you?"
said the crow.
"We have a maid and a cook,"
said the rooster.
"What can you be?"

"I can be the butler,"
said the crow.

"That is a fine idea,"
said the hen.
"Climb in!" said the rooster
to the crow.
"Cock-a-doodle-do!"
The rooster, the hen,
the sparrow and the duck
made room in the shoe
for the crow.
The mice travelled on.

At the edge of the woods
they met a fox.
"And who do I have
the pleasure of meeting
on this lonely road?"
said the fox.
The rooster puffed himself up.
"How do you do, sir," he said.
"My wife and I
are going to the city.
I will be king
and she will be my queen.
These are my butler, our cook,
our maid and our horses."

"Yum," said the fox to himself.
"What delicious company!"
 Out loud he said,
"My dear king and queen,
 the city is far away.
 Darkness is falling.
 Stay and rest for a while
 in my humble home.
 We will have supper."

"Thank you, my good sir,"
said the rooster.
He stepped out of the shoe
and walked into the house.
The hen, the sparrow,
the duck and the crow
followed after him.

When the birds were all inside,
the fox said,
"Will you sing to me, your majesty,
before I eat my supper?"

The rooster puffed himself up.
He was ready to crow.

The sparrow saw that something
was very wrong.
There were five guests for dinner,
and the table was set for only one.
"Wait!" she cried.
"The king cannot sing.
This room is too stuffy.
All the windows are closed."

"I will open the window,"
said the fox.
I am very hungry, he thought.
He ran to the window
and opened it.

The sparrow flew up
on the windowsill.
"Follow me," she cried,
"and fly away
as fast as you can!"

"Help!" cried the rooster.

"We're in danger!" cried the hen.

"Follow me!" cried the sparrow.

The crow, the duck,

the hen and the rooster

flew through the window.

They jumped into the shoe.

"Cock-a-doodle-do!

Cock-a-doodle-do!"

cried the rooster.

The mice galloped away very fast.

43

They did not stop

until they were back on the farm.

"I do not want to be
a maid any more,"
said the sparrow.
She flew away.
"Being a butler is not for me,"
said the crow.
He flew away.
"I really cannot cook,"
said the duck.
She flew away.

"To be a queen
is very dangerous,"
said the hen.
"Cock-a-doodle-do!"
crowed the rooster.

They began to peck
and scratch
in the ground.

And the mice made a nest
in the shoe.

— ◆ —

ANITA LOBEL was born in Cracow, Poland, just before the beginning of the Second World War. In the Jewish household in which she lived there were several servants, including a nanny for the children. It was this strong-willed Catholic peasant who saved the lives of Anita and her brother during the war, passing them off as her own children.

They spent five years being carted from one town to another, until finally they were discovered and taken to a concentration camp. Somehow they survived until the Liberation, when they were taken to Sweden. There they were reunited with their parents and set off for a new life in America.

Anita became a textile designer and

married the author-illustrator Arnold Lobel.
Seeing fabrics which Anita had designed,
Arnold's editor suggested she illustrate a
picture book. The result was Anita Lobel's
first book, *Sven's Bridge*. This has been
followed by dozens of picture books –
amongst them *On Market Street*, *A Treeful of
Pigs*, and *How the Rooster Saved the Day*, all
written by Arnold and illustrated by Anita –
and by several notable honours, including the
Boston Globe-Horn Book Honor Book and
the Caldecott Honor Book awards.

Arnold and Anita's daughter has already
illustrated two children's books, and an
exciting new venture has been *Once:
A Lullaby*, illustrated by Anita and set to
music by her son Adam.